C000015830

Stocking Fillers
Twelve Short Stories for Christmas

Debbie Young

Hawkesbury Press

Contents

PREFACE

I've written these Christmas stories to provide readers with comic relief from the inevitable stresses of the festive season. Unlike many Christmas stories, mine are not steeped in sugar, and not all the characters are entirely likeable, but all the same I hope they'll make you smile.

Whether you choose to read just one story on each of the traditional Twelve Days of Christmas, or to wolf them all down in a single sitting, I'm hoping that you'll enjoy *Stocking Fillers* – even if after reading it, you may never view Christmas in quite the same way again.

However you plan to celebrate this festive season, I wish you peace, love and joy.

Debbie Young

The Christmas Letter

*D*ear Friends and Relations

I expect you're wondering why this year's Christmas letter is coming from me rather than the wife. The good news is that it will therefore be free of spelling mistakes and grammatical gaffes. That's just the first surprise in our household's 2014 round up.

First, news of the offspring.

You will doubtless recall from Trudy's last Christmas letter, if she did a proper job of it, that our elder one, Caroline, was due to sit her A Level examinations this summer. Unfortunately I was the only one who took this challenge seriously. Painstakingly I prepared revision spreadsheets and progress graphs to direct her preparations. If only she had taken more notice of her father than of that inadequate boyfriend, Jake (or perhaps his name is James), she might have achieved the straight As I'd hoped for, instead of her feeble three Bs. She seemed not to care that this dismal performance would not get her into the medical school that I'd been planning for her since the day she was born. How she could throw away such a valuable prospect in favour of the performing arts, of all things, I do not understand. That is why I refused to go to Speech Day, *where the only prizes she received were for worthless extra-curricular activities such as drama. If you ask me, she has wasted far too much time starring in school plays throughout her secondary education.*

I assumed her poor example would make young David buck his ideas up on entering the Lower Sixth in September, which indeed he needed to do if he is to have any chance of a career in Law. However he continued to fritter his time away on his wretched guitar. His uncanny ability to gain bookings for his band to perform live in pubs will certainly not fit him to succeed at the Bar. Neither the band's success in some half-witted television talent show nor the resulting recording contract will convince me that he has not been wasting his time.

Sadly, Trudy has been of very little help in keeping our children on the straight and narrow, being too deeply immersed in her own selfish interests. Since she started volunteering at that dreadful women's refuge in March, she has lost all sight of her priorities. Very often there is not even a meal awaiting my return from the office. When I have asked her to explain why she bothers working there at all when I am perfectly able to provide for all her needs, she has not been forthcoming. Her entire conversation these days consists of regurgitating the opinions of some fool called Adam (or is it Adrian?) who runs the place. I assume the inane smile constantly on her face is caused by the contrast between her pleasant home life and the wretched state of those she works with.

As for me, my continuing endeavours in the City have earned me a further promotion this year. My annual bonus was the largest I've ever received. It seemed only fair to treat myself to a new sports car on the proceeds – a two-seater Porsche 911 GT3, which features a six-cylinder naturally aspirated engine capable of as much as 500 HP, a top speed of 198 mph and 0-60 acceleration of 3.5 seconds. Never let it be said that, in my career and as head of the household, I do not continue to set a good example for my family.

You can therefore imagine my surprise when I discovered that each member of my family had made separate plans for the festive season. Caroline, rejected of course by medical school, has set off with a travelling theatre company for a tour of Europe. When Trudy took a phone call from her last night, the girl revealed that by Christmas she would be in Turkey. Trudy laughed and said, "What a suitable place to spend Christmas." I do not see why as it is 99 per cent Muslim.

David, meanwhile, will be spending the school holidays performing in London with his band, paid for and, I hope, supervised by the television company. I remain deeply concerned about his attitude to his studies: he left behind the revision bag of schoolbooks that I had carefully packed for him.

In their absence, Trudy has now announced that she'll be working at the refuge throughout the Christmas holidays. Apparently Alan (or is it Andrew?) was especially keen to have her there. You'd think at her age she'd know better than to put up with such obvious bullying. Anyone would think she was the homeless one.

I am therefore writing to you now, my dear friends and relations, to offer you the opportunity to have me spend the festive season with you. I'm afraid I won't be able to satisfy you all, so it must be first come, first served. I apologise in advance to those who will inevitably be disappointed. I look forward to sharing more Christmas cheer with you.

I anticipate your prompt reply.

Yours sincerely

Charles

I'm Dreaming of a
Green Christmas

"I'm really pleased with how I've done my Christmas cards this year," explained Julia, biting into a carrot stick. "Not only have I recycled last year's cards by cutting off the front, I've also saved on envelopes. Instead of sticking the picture on to another card, I've just drawn a line down the back. Then I've used them like postcards, writing my greeting on the left and the address on the right. Don't you think that's a good idea?"

She gazed at Marcus hopefully, keen to show him that for their first Christmas together she was embracing his environmental ideals.

"It's brilliant. I think you should patent it."

With a little sigh of happiness, Julia dipped the rest of her carrot stick into the hummus pot that was balanced between them on the bench. She knew he wouldn't mind. They were long past the stage of worrying about sharing germs.

"And instead of wasting wrapping paper, I've bought reusable shopping bags. I'm going to put everyone's presents in a cloth bag with a bit of tinsel – no, holly – around the handles to make it look festive."

Nodding approval, Marcus pulled a conspicuously straight banana, the type rejected by supermarkets for insufficient curve, out of his pocket. He didn't really like bananas, but always packed a straight one in his lunch bag as a matter of principle.

"That's very good. You can never have too many bags-for-life."

"As for the presents, I've sourced them all from charity shops – either that or re-gifted unwanted presents that I had for my birthday last month."

"Well, I hope you'll like the present I've got for you," he replied, setting down his untasted banana on his empty tofu wrapper. "As this is our last lunch together before we go off to our respective folks for the holidays, I thought I'd give it to you now. Is that OK?"

Inwardly Julia cringed at the reminder that he hadn't suggested they spend the holidays together, but she knew it made sense not to rush him if he was unsure. Nor, to be honest, did she really want to spend Christmas away from her own family.

"Yes, of course, that's fine."

She hadn't wanted to risk repeating the embarrassing episode of the previous Christmas, when she'd given her former boyfriend, Tom, an expensive camera and received nothing in return. Surreptitiously Julia patted her coat pocket in which she'd hidden Marcus's present from her, a solar-powered wristwatch made from recycled CDs, and gave a nervous laugh.

"I bet it's something environmentally friendly!" she said brightly, regretting that it was unlikely to be perfume, her favourite kind of gift.

Marcus smiled.

"How well you know me! Yes, it's definitely environmentally friendly. It's even in a recycled box."

Julia's heart sank a little further, thinking of the gifts she had been popping into cloth bags the night before. The only one in a box was a bottle of shower gel.

"It's what you might call pre-owned," said Marcus, undoing the zip of his inside coat pocket. "Or, to be more poetic, pre-loved."

Julia gave a flicker of a smile. You couldn't exactly pre-love shower gel. Maybe it was going to be OK after all. She ventured a guess to disperse her tension.

"So it's not edible?"

"Nope. At least, you wouldn't eat it on purpose, though I've heard of girls accidentally swallowing one in a glass of champagne."

She played for time, not daring to believe what she thought he meant. Marcus paused, gazing across the empty park to consider.

"So not something to read? A second-hand book?"

"No, the only way you could read it would be in a psychic way, like a crystal ball, if you're into that sort of thing – staring into its shiny facets to see your future."

He flashed his most winning smile, green eyes twinkling. A shiver ran down Julia's spine as the significance of his words sank in. Her jaw dropped ever so slightly open, and she raised her hand to mask her mouth for fear of emitting a squeal. Facets – wasn't that the technical term for the cut surfaces of a diamond?

"Can I – can I wear it?" she almost whispered, still not daring to believe it might be something that would ensure they'd spend all their future Christmases together. His only answer was a self-satisfied grin as he finally fished out of his pocket a small black leather ring box. Slowly, teasingly, he opened the lid to reveal a diamond solitaire.

This time, Julia could not contain her excitement as he removed it from its navy velvet cushion. "Oh, Marcus, it's beautiful! That's the perfect Christmas present!"

She flung her arms round his neck and buried her face in his long, dark curls. Then, calming herself, she let go and sat back on the bench, holding out both hands for him to choose a finger. After all, there was a chance that he didn't mean it to be an engagement ring. She didn't want to embarrass herself by jumping to the wrong conclusion.

To her delight, Marcus lifted her left hand, selected her wedding finger and slid the ring gently into place. As if touched by Christmas magic, it was the perfect fit.

"So I take it that's a yes, then?" said Marcus, holding on to her left hand with both of his. "Julia, will you marry me?"

"Oh, Marcus, YES!" cried Julia. "I love it! I love you! Darling, it's wonderful!" It was the first time she had let herself call him darling. She stared at her outstretched left hand, trying to digest the truth. "But it's so extravagant. It must have cost the earth. You shouldn't have!"

Marcus shook his head confidently. "Don't worry about that, sweetheart. You're worth it, and my conscience is clear. As I'm sure you'll appreciate, it's actually recycled. It's the same ring that I gave my first fiancée."

He squeezed her hand proprietorially. The strength of her returning grip startled him as she replied.

"Oh Marcus, you really shouldn't have!"

Do You Believe?

"**Y**ou're doing it all wrong. You know that, don't you?" was the opening gambit of the last small boy to come into my grotto today.

The dark-haired, dark-eyed child sat down on the stool at my feet for his allocated three minutes. As he gazed earnestly at me through his round dark-rimmed glasses, the reflection of the fairy lights twinkled on the surface of his black lace-up shoes, which were surprisingly shiny for this end of the school day. I wondered whether he'd polished them specially in preparation for his visit.

"This is Jerome," said Samantha brightly. "Jerome is nine. Hello, Jerome."

Samantha is my afternoon elf. I have Caroline in the morning, but she only works during the school day. Henderson's is very good like that, flexible with its workers' shifts. That's how they get decent Christmas staff.

Behind Jerome's back, Samantha winked at me as she upended the egg timer for his visit.

"What do you mean, I'm doing it all wrong? How do you make that out, sonny?"

"Well." Jerome gazed at the floor for a moment, as if planning a long speech. "You're what my dad calls a last-minute man. Doing everything at the last minute. My dad's very good at planning ahead. He's what they call a time management consultant."

"Is he, now?"

"Yes. My dad says that if my mum didn't leave everything till the last minute, she wouldn't be rushing around so much now. I think you're a lot like my mum. If you were a bit better at planning things, you wouldn't have to be up all night on Christmas Eve. You could just do a little bit of work every day all through the year instead."

Samantha clapped her hand over her mouth to suppress a giggle. She does that a lot, does Samantha.

"Really? And how would that work?"

"You could do what my grandma does. She's my dad's mum. Instead of trying to do all her shopping just before Christmas, she starts buying presents in the January sales. Dad says my mum ought to do what Grandma does."

"I bet that goes down a storm with your mum."

Jerome's brow furrowed briefly before he continued. "It's much cheaper that way, because you can get things really cheap in the sales. And you don't have to buy everything all at once, so you don't run out of money like Mum does."

"Really?"

"Yes. It's obvious, really."

The little boy looked so earnest that I tried to convince myself he meant well. Then I spotted a flaw in his logic.

"But how would I know what to buy? Children don't usually send me their letters till December."

Jerome shrugged. "Some children will probably ask for things that you've bought in the sales"

I had to admit he had a point.

"And there's bound to be some who just say they want a surprise. That's what my little sister always says. Just give them whatever you've got left. Easy."

Samantha was flicking a duster over the fake fireplace, one of the afternoon elf's duties at the end of the day. "Not much gets past you, Jerome, does it, eh?" she encouraged him.

Jerome solemnly shook his head.

"Then you'd have more time to wrap everything, too," he continued. "And to sort it all out into different delivery sacks. You could do one for each country. By the way, you might want to think about posting some of the presents instead of trying to take them all round to people's houses on Christmas Eve. You're lucky the animal rights people haven't told you off for making those reindeer work so hard."

This boy was too clever by half. Conscious that the egg-timer had long since run out, I tried to steer him back on track.

"So what would you like for Christmas, Jerome? I'm guessing that you've been a good boy this year."

He nodded. "Of course. It makes much more sense to be good and get lots of presents. I worked that out a long time ago. Anyway, I put everything I wanted in my Christmas letter to you, don't you remember? I sent it to you shortly after Easter."

I clapped my hand to my brow as if recovering from a momentary memory lapse.

"Yes, of course," I replied. "So why did you come to see me today?"

"Just to give advice. Besides, it would seem rude not to call in while I was passing, after you've gone to the trouble of stopping off here at your busiest time of year."

"Seems fair enough," I said. "Thanks for dropping by."

Jerome stood up and stretched out his hand to shake mine. It made a refreshing change from a hug.

"It's a pleasure, Santa. Thanks for everything."

"Thank you, Jerome."

And with that he skipped off towards the exit.

"Was he taking the piss?" I hissed to the smiling Samantha. "Do you think he's stopped believing in Santa and was just having a laugh at my expense? Honestly, as if this job isn't tiring enough without having to contend with smart Alecs!"

Samantha shushed me, her finger to her lips, and nodded towards the exit to indicate the boy's return.

"Sorry, Santa, I forgot to say – my sister's at ballet so she couldn't come to see you herself, but she told me to remind you that she's asked for a surprise. In her letter. Which I made her send at Easter, when I sent you mine."

I peered at him over my glasses. "Jerome, what a wise and thoughtful boy you are. Are you for real?"

He looked at me quizzically for a moment then burst out laughing. "Oh, Santa, you are funny! Of course I am. I'm just as real as you are."

I glanced across to Samantha, still unsure he wasn't taking me for a ride.

"See you Christmas Eve, then," Jerome finished. "You know where I live."

With a final shake of my hand, he ran off and out into the big, wide world. I hoped it was ready for him.

The Revolting Toys

"**M**illy, if you don't tidy your room, there'll be no Christmas presents for you!"

When Milly's mother, Kate, said "tidy", what she really meant was "thoroughly rationalise your bedroom, put away any toys that you still play with, and bag up the rest for the charity shop". But even the simple shorthand of "tidy" did not register with ten-year-old Milly. In her over-crowded jumble of a bedroom there were always much more interesting things to do. She was currently engineering a complex plaited hairstyle on a grubby naked Barbie.

It's uncanny, thought Kate, hoovering around a teetering pile of board games. Milly always starts playing with anything I'm thinking of taking to the charity shop. It's as if she has some special power to stop me blitzing the room myself.

Her gaze fell on a 50-piece jigsaw, marked as suitable for 5-7 year olds. Surely Milly would never open that box again? Kate added it to the pile of games and looked about her. How much bigger the room would seem if tidy, how much nicer for entertaining Milly's friends. Just what was it that was holding Milly back from tidying up? Fear of change? Kate knew all kids were averse to change, but something had to give or else there would be no space to store this year's Christmas presents.

Treading painfully on a piece of Lego as she hauled the vacuum cleaner down the stairs, Kate decided to leave a pile of charity collection bags in Milly's bedroom as a last-ditch hint. If they were still empty on Christmas Eve, she'd take them away and leave Milly to muddle through the mess on her own.

***

That night, when Kate was downstairs watching a DVD with her husband Pete, and Milly was fast asleep in bed, a small mauve teddy bear named Lupin emerged from under the bed where he'd lain unnoticed for over a year.

"Look, folks, here's a way out of this mess at last." He pointed to the pile of empty charity bags that lay in the middle of the rug. "Which good cause do you lot want to help? The PDSA gets my vote."

Lupin opened a blue and white bag and hopped inside. "I've always wanted to work with animals," he remarked, making himself comfortable.

Rosa, a tousle-haired blue-eyed brunette doll, crawled out of the dressing-up box. "I'd like to Save the Children, but I'm not going without a change of clothes." She reached under Milly's dressing table and hauled out a red toy suitcase. "Let's see: a coat, a jumper, a hat and scarf, a couple of frocks..."

As Rosa rifled among the dolls' clothes, a baby doll, her face discoloured with green and purple crayon, snatched a toy bottle of milk from the top of the pile. "Well, I might get hungry on the way," she said, ignoring the brunette's disapproving look.

"What about something to do on the journey? I do like a nice jigsaw," piped up a plush giraffe, stretching its neck straight for the first time in the six months since it had been shoved under the bookshelves. "Maybe I'll take this harmonica, so we can have a sing-song."

"Something to read would be handy," replied an orange elephant, curling its trunk around a board book.

Soon Milly's bedroom was a hive of activity as numerous cuddly toys and dolls methodically packed themselves and their carefully selected luggage into the charity bags. Only the few that had a close bond with Milly held back, though they did help the emigrants on their way. Hazel, a toy rabbit so cherished that her stuffing had compacted round her middle, climbed down the steps from the cabin bed where she'd been dozing in Milly's arms and neatly tied the tops of the full bags. With the assistance of Carrie, Milly's favourite doll that was the size of a toddler, Hazel dragged the bags out onto the landing. Before mounting the ladder to rejoin Milly, Hazel gazed around the tidy bedroom with satisfaction.

"That's much better," she declared. "So much nicer for those of us who are staying. And much better for the others to go somewhere where they'll be better appreciated."

She hopped up the wooden steps to snuggle back in Milly's arms. The child woke up just enough to nuzzle into Hazel's soft fur and give a little sigh of satisfaction. Soon both were fast asleep.

***

When Kate came up to bed, she was astonished to see the pile of plump charity bags stacked neatly on the landing.

"Well, she did that quietly, though I suppose the film we were watching was pretty noisy," she remarked to Pete. "I can't be cross with her for sneaking out of bed after bedtime if that's the result."

"I told you she'd do it herself eventually if you just stopped nagging her," he replied.

***

Next morning, when Kate went into Milly's room to wake her, she found her daughter sitting up in bed, gazing around the room with a look of delight on her face.

"Wow, my bedroom looks so much bigger now!" said Milly.

Kate narrowed her eyes. "You're happy with it like this, then?"

"Oh yes, Mum, it's so much nicer." Milly threw back the duvet and slid down the short ladder to the floor. "Thanks, Mum, I knew you'd tidy it for me if I put it off long enough."

"Whatever do you mean?" asked Kate, but Milly, already on her way to the bathroom with Hazel the bunny wedged firmly under her arm, didn't hear her mum.

Too grateful for the tidy state of the room to quiz her daughter further, Kate returned to the landing to whisk the bags down to the car. She thought she'd better drop them off at the charity shop straight away, in case Milly should change her mind. As she heaved them into the boot, the top of one bag came undone, and a fluffy-haired doll's head poked out.

"Oh, Suzy, not you!" Kate cried, retrieving the grubby doll from the bag. "You were Milly's first ever doll. We can't get rid of you. Not yet."

She parted the ripped plastic further and peered inside.

"Daisy! Grandma bought you for Milly on her very first day at school. We ought to hang on to you."

Tucking Suzy and Daisy under one arm, Kate slammed the car boot shut before her resolve could weaken. She thought she might just manage to sneak them back into the toy-box before Milly came out of the bathroom. After all, Christmas wouldn't be the same without them.

Park and Ride

As Santa approached the bus stop, he thanked his lucky stars that this was the last night of wearing his ridiculous suit for a while. In two days' time, he'd be back in his comfy Blakes' uniform, sticking "reduced" stickers on the Toy Department's seasonal goods to shift them in the post-Christmas sale.

He shivered and pulled his red jacket more closely about him. The number of staff in the queue reassured him that he hadn't missed the last bus. Only staff were left at the mall at this hour, the punters having all been chucked out at closing time.

"Hello, Santa! We don't usually see you here, do we?"

Vicky from Perfumes clacked along the pavement towards him in high heels, pancake make-up shiny after a day under the bright lights of her department. Walking through Perfumes always made Santa squint after spending all day in his dimly lit grotto.

"No, I don't usually use the Park and Ride. My wife generally drops me off and picks me up right outside the mall, but she was a bit busy today so I took the car myself."

Vicky collapsed gratefully onto one of the bus shelter's hard plastic seats and slipped off her shoes to rub her feet. "I've had a busy day myself, actually. All those men rushing in at the last minute, expecting me magically to know their wives' perfumes from their description!"

She winked at him, and he patted his bulging left pocket, in which he'd stashed a gift-wrapped bottle of Chanel Number 5 not half an hour before.

"Still, couple of days off now, eh?" he consoled her, "before the madness starts all over again."

"Not for you though, surely, Santa? You've got the busiest night of the year ahead of you."

"Yep, a busy night with my feet up in front of the fire, a nice bottle of Shiraz and a plate of my wife's home-made mince pies."

A squeal of brakes heralded the arrival of the last Park and Ride bus of the night as it came down the ramp from the main road. As it drew to a halt by the bus stop, the doors hissed open, and Santa stood back to let the earlier arrivals get on before him, followed by Vicky, high heels still in her hand. Just as he was about to ascend the step himself, there came a sharp shout from behind him. "Hey, wait for me!"

Another white-bearded man in a red suit was attempting to sprint from the direction of Parkers', the upmarket department store at the far end of the precinct. He clearly wasn't built for running.

"It's alright, take your time," called the driver amiably, his benevolent mood fostered by double pay for working late on Christmas Eve. He turned to Santa. "Looks like you've got competition."

"One of my clones," Santa replied amiably. "You don't think I can really get round the world in one night on my own, do you?"

"Not on my bus you won't. I'm all done after this trip."

Santa settled himself into the first empty double seat, from where he watched his doppelganger climb aboard and show the driver his ticket.

"Wouldn't do for Santa to miss the last bus home, would it?" the driver asked him.

"I'm not Santa, I'm Father Christmas," came the breathless reply. "We do things the old-fashioned way where I work."

As Father Christmas sat down heavily beside Santa, the doors hissed closed and the bus lurched away from the stop.

"Long day?" Santa asked him. As Father Christmas nodded, Santa took in the superior quality of his rival's uniform. Leather boots instead of wellies, thick woollen suit, and fluffier fur around the edges. Parkers' department store clearly had a more generous staff uniform than his own employer, Blakes'. The beard was much more realistic too. Santa touched the acrylic ringlets beneath his own chin. No real beard could be that curly.

"I can never believe quite how many parents bring their kids in on the last day," continued Santa. "I mean, supposing the kid tells me that they want something the parents haven't bought. It's a bit late for them to put it right."

"I'd rather see them late in December than in November," said Father Christmas, breathing more easily now. "That never feels quite the same to me. I'm a bit of a traditionalist, to be honest."

Santa nodded. "Still, sometimes it's better to make changes. This year, I got my departmental manager to change the way the grotto offers presents. The kids just used to get what they were given. Now they can choose from a range laid out on a table, unwrapped, so they're sure of getting something they'll like. We even include store gift cards to the value of the grotto entry fee. No wonder we've been busier than ever this year. Smart marketing, that's what it is, even if I do say so myself."

Father Christmas sighed. "Ha, marketing! Profit and loss, share-holders' interests, customer satisfaction. Those things don't sit well with what Father Christmas is really about."

Santa pulled a mobile phone out of his pocket, quickly typed a text to this wife ("I'm on the bus") and hit the send button. "You have to wonder about olden days, though," he said, tucking the phone back in his pocket. "Apparently I used to mete out punishments as well as presents. Santa carried a stick to beat the kids who'd been bad."

"That'll be St Nicholas, in Holland," said Father Christmas, grabbing the handrail to stop himself sliding off the seat as the bus swung round the corner into the car park, "with his accomplice, Black Pete."

"I'd rather spend my days in a cosy grotto with my pretty young elf than Black Pete," replied Santa. "Better not tell that to the wife."

With a smile, Father Christmas hauled himself upright, putting his bulging stomach on a level with Santa's eye line. *That belly's the real thing,* thought the latter, pleased that he could only achieve the required profile with the aid of a pillow.

"Got far to go now?" asked Father Christmas as they descended the bus steps together.

"Only a couple of miles. And I got lucky with a parking space this morning. That's me right here." He stopped by a black Fiat Panda and reached in his pocket for the keys. "So, have a good one, chief. Maybe see you next year?"

"Not if I see you first!" said Father Christmas with a jovial wink, before turning to stroll slowly across the now nearly empty car park. When he reached the far corner, he turned to check that every last car had gone and watched the procession of taillights behind the trundling bus.

He then ducked behind the storage shed, where he'd left his own vehicle tucked out of sight for security reasons. After all, it was rather heavily laden in preparation for the night ahead.

"OK, lads, off we go. The serious work of the day is just beginning."

Climbing aboard, he shook the reins to guide the reindeer out of hiding, turning them to face the empty car park.

"Hi, hi!" he cried to set the reindeer into a run. Using the empty car park as a runway, Father Christmas settled back comfortably as the sleigh began its ascent into the starry night sky.

Christmas Time

M y annual Christmas present from my godmother, Auntie Fay, may be small in size because she has to post it all the way from Australia, but it's always a tonic that helps me get through the whirlwind of preparing for a typical family Christmas.

No surprise, then, that I can't resist opening her parcel the moment it arrives. This year, it landed on my doormat on 23 December. Seeing her beautiful copperplate handwriting on the label beneath the showy Australian stamps made my heart skip a beat with excitement. Settling down at the kitchen table, I peeled off the outer wrapper to reveal a small Christmas card bent protectively around a tiny square parcel. I ripped off the glittery paper, sending specks of silver fluttering up around me as if heralding a magic spell. To my surprise, inside lay nothing more remarkable than a slim alarm clock. Its circular clock face bore a stylised world map, reminding me of just how much distance lay between Auntie Fay and me. Around the edge of the clock face ran the slogan "Stop the world!" repeated several times.

I flipped the clock over to see whether it was made in Australia, but found no clue. There were just the usual knobs, time set and alarm set, and three buttons labelled off, stop and snooze. I adjusted it to English time, then twiddled the alarm set knob to match the time so that I could check out the sound of the alarm. It was a pleasantly low vibrating purr that I didn't think would be audible beyond my side of the bed. Then I noticed a raised pillow-shaped symbol with an arrow pointing to it, suggesting that the clock should be tucked under the pillow for the gentlest, most comforting of awakenings. I liked the sound of that.

Feeling vaguely guilty that, like a badly brought-up child, I'd taken stock of the present before the card, I set the clock down on the kitchen table and opened the card. It showed an unlikely scene of a wombat and a kangaroo exchanging Christmas gifts. What would they buy each other? I wondered. Inside, opposite the printed greeting, the page was filled edge to edge with Auntie Fay's handwriting, its neat script at odds with the rambling message. She always wrote exactly as she talked.

"Jessie my dear, I hope this little gift will help you get more rest and catch up with yourself. I couldn't help noticing you looked a little tired in that last lovely photo you sent me of you and Jake and your dear boys, haven't they grown? More like your father every day, that's no bad thing, he's a dear boy too, at least he was when we were small, though always bigger than me, of course. Don't try to do too much at this busy time of year, will you? Get plenty of sleep and you'll all enjoy Christmas so much more. Those buttons on the back are there for a reason, you know, so make sure you use them!"

I put Auntie Fay's card on the kitchen dresser, where it could stand in proxy for her throughout the season's celebrations. Then I went upstairs to slip her gift under my pillow before getting on with my chores.

***

By bedtime I was bleary eyed from a long day of channelling the twins' excitement into constructive behaviour. We really didn't need quite so many paper chains, but making them keeps six-year-olds occupied for ages. I flung myself wearily into bed, forgetting Auntie Fay's new clock until I fluffed up the pillows for a soothing late-night read. I showed the clock to Jake, who was sitting up in bed playing Hearts on his tablet.

"That's cute," he remarked. "But surely you're not planning to set an alarm for tomorrow, are you? We're on holiday! A fortnight without work, hurrah!"

"Are you kidding? I've still got all the presents to wrap, mince pies to make, vegetables to peel, stuffing to mix, plus loads of cleaning to do so the house looks half decent for when our folks come round for Christmas dinner. The kids are messing the house up faster than I can tidy. In fact, even if I didn't go to bed at all tonight, I'd still have trouble fitting everything in.

Jake set the tablet on his bedside table, leaned over to give me a quick kiss, then lay down facing away from me.

"Well, wake me up when you've finished, love. I'm on holiday. Night night."

I set Auntie Fay's alarm for 7am and slipped it under my pillow.

***

I woke up to its gentle purring what seemed like moments later. The light was still on, my reading book had fallen sideways in my hand, and there was just enough traffic roaring past the house to confirm that the rush hour was about to begin.

Hazy with insufficient sleep, I pulled the clock out from under my pillow, flipped it over and hit a button on the back to silence the purr. Jake slumbered on peacefully as I threw back the duvet and wrapped my dressing gown around me. The refreshing silence from across the landing told me that, by some miracle, the twins were also still asleep. I stuffed my feet into fluffy slippers and stumbled downstairs to brew a sustaining pot of tea. I needed to be fortified before I tackled my to-do list.

I decided first to take advantage of the continuing peace upstairs to wrap all the presents. Job done, I hid them in the ironing basket (the last place Jake or the boys would think to look) before taking a cup of tea up to Jake. He was still spark out, as were the boys, so I left the tea on his bedside table. As I went back downstairs, I slipped one hand into my dressing gown pocket in search of a tissue, only to discover that I'd absent-mindedly put Auntie Fay's clock in there instead of putting it back under my pillow. Turning it over to check the time, I realised with a start that it still said seven o'clock. Had I inadvertently dislodged the battery? No, it was still ticking. So why had the hands not moved on?

But I couldn't spare the time to investigate, so I tucked it back into my pocket and hauled the Dyson out of the broom cupboard. The noise of vacuuming would certainly wake the boys, but it had to be done. Yet as I tucked the Dyson back in the cupboard half an hour later, there was still no sound from upstairs. Suddenly filled with panic, I ran upstairs to check the boys were still breathing. They were, but they were asleep, so I tiptoed back downstairs to start cooking.

Not used to such peace in the mornings, I clicked on the radio for company. I was just in time to hear the BBC's pips marking the hour, immediately followed by the announcement of the seven o'clock news headlines. Spooked, I quickly pressed the off switch. Surely I'd done at least three hours' work since Auntie Fay's alarm woke me up at seven? For a moment I wondered whether it had reverted to Australian time, but that made no sense because the time difference between our countries is more like twelve hours than three.

I distracted myself by setting to work on the mountain of vegetables that I planned to prepare and leave in the fridge, ready to cook on Christmas Day. That job done, I started on the mince pies.

By the time the third batch was cooling on the wire rack I was feeling peckish, so I made another pot of tea and some toast. I thought I'd take Jake a fresh cup. When I nipped upstairs to get his mug, predictably still untouched, I was astonished to find that the tea in it was still as hot as when I'd poured it hours before. It was as if time had stood still.

I sat down on the bed with a thump, not caring whether I disturbed Jake now, and drew Auntie Fay's alarm clock out of my dressing gown pocket. I didn't need to look at it to know that it would still say 7am. I turned it over to double-check which button I'd hit to turn off the alarm. One was still depressed. It was the stop button. And then it hit me: with my Stop the World clock, I'd stopped the world.

I had a sudden panic. Was the action reversible? Quickly I hit the stop button again, and as it sprang back up the second hand started to move. At the very same moment Jake awoke.

"Is that my tea? Thanks, love. Happy Christmas Eve!"

All at once, from the twins' bedroom came sounds of excitable boys on the cusp of their seventh Christmas. Having already completed my chores for the day, I realised to my delight that I could now relax and enjoy the day with them.

***

By the evening, I was in a mellow mood and unusually calm while bathing the twins and putting them to bed. Then Jake and I enjoyed a relaxing evening watching television with a jug of mulled wine. While Jake was out of the room on a quest for Pringles, I raised a silent toast of gratitude to Auntie Fay for her thoughtful, magical gift of time.

My gratitude to her did not end there. I'd told the boys they were not allowed to wake us on Christmas morning until six o'clock. I had the foresight to set Auntie Fay's alarm clock for one minute before six. The moment I felt its gentle purr, I slipped my hand beneath my pillow and felt for the stop button. Then I turned over, snuggled down under the duvet and leaned in to the warmth of Jake's back. Plenty of time yet for a nice lie-in. Christmas Day wouldn't begin until I was good and ready. Smiling, I closed my eyes.

The Groundhog Christmas

"**B**loody Christmas lists!"

Meryl was totting up the cost of her nine-year-old son Jacob's wish list, shaking her head at the spelling. "You'd think he'd know by now that there's only one G in Lego," she muttered. "There's enough of it in his bedroom."

She crossed off items that couldn't easily be bought at the mall. Even without the time machine and the helicopter, the list totalled over £200.

"It's not as if he hasn't already got most of this stuff," she remarked to her husband, John, who was immersed in the daily paper's Sudoku puzzle.

"Mmm?"

"I mean, how much Lego does a boy need? His bedroom's got more Lego than a Lego shop. Would he even notice if there was more of it? Or if I took some of it out?" She threw the list down on the coffee table, her pencil clattering after it. "How long do you think it would take me to empty his bedroom of Lego if I removed one brick at a time? I reckon I wouldn't live long enough. I swear there are some kits in there that he's never even opened – that police car kit he had last Christmas, for example. I don't know why I bother."

"Mmm."

"And Molly's just as bad." Meryl produced Molly's dog-eared list from the back pocket of her jeans. "She's asked for Barbies and Barbie clothes. Her Barbies have got more clothes than the Queen. Why does she want more? They've got no character. They're all clones. What's the point?"

Meryl scrutinised the non-Barbie section for a moment. "And colouring pencils. And paints. And craft kits. If she did nothing but draw and paint till the day she leaves home, she still wouldn't use them all up."

After scribbling the final number in the Sudoku grid, John threw the paper and pen down on the coffee table and glanced at his watch with a smirk. "Yes! New personal best. Fastest Sudoku I've ever done. Now, what's your problem?"

Meryl sighed. "It should not be MY problem. OUR problem is the kids' Christmas lists. Why can't YOU just take some responsibility for them for once? It's all either impossible stuff – Molly wants a flying carpet for her bedroom – or stuff that they've already got and don't appreciate."

John extricated Molly's sticky list from between Meryl's fingers and perused it. "What's wrong with a brown and white puppy?" he queried. "Our carpets are brown and white. That should be fine."

Meryl sighed again. "You just don't get it, do you? I spend my life picking up toys and putting them away. All Christmas does is add to my workload."

John shrugged again. "Then don't buy them anything. Simple." He picked up his empty coffee cup and stared into it. Taking it from his hand, Meryl heaved herself up from the sofa and went to the kitchen to flick down the switch on the kettle.

"That's easy for you to say! What about their little faces on Christmas morning?"

"Well, what about the stuff they had last year that's still unopened? Recycle it. Sneak it out of their rooms and rewrap it. The only new stuff you need buy is a couple of big cardboard boxes for them to play with on Christmas afternoon. We could spend what we save on a new big telly. In fact, they could play with the box the big telly comes in. There you go, problem solved."

Spooning coffee granules too quickly into the cup, Meryl scattered them across the damp worktop where they expanded, fizzing. But as she stirred in the milk, her hand steadied and she started to formulate her master plan.

***

A month later, while the kids were out of her way watching the BBC's Christmas Eve family movie, Meryl smiled as she rewrapped familiar presents in her bedroom. Before the kids had broken up from school, she'd managed to sneak plenty of suitable presents out of their bedrooms, each item barely touched since they'd been ripped out of last year's Christmas gift wrap. She was looking forward to seeing the Christmas specials on the new big television too. In high spirits, she coerced the children to bed after the film. Back downstairs in the kitchen, she sang Christmas carols as she filled their stockings with fruit and sweets, the only items she'd had to buy. She'd found a bag of foil-wrapped chocolate coins that had been lurking in the larder all year.

"Well, I have to say, my conscience is clear," she announced to John, sinking down beside him on the leather sofa, glass of Pinot in hand. "They've got practically everything they asked for, so they can't complain. I'm very pleased."

John smiled and set his beer glass down on the coffee table. "And me, love. Well done."

As Meryl repositioned the beer glass on a coaster, John reached for the remote control of the new giant television.

***

Next morning, the children awoke before dawn and stuffed themselves with stocking sweets until 7am, the earliest that they were allowed to wake their parents.

"Come on, Mum, let's go!" cried Molly, thumping her parents' cream duvet with a chocolatey hand before racing her brother down the stairs.

As Meryl rose slowly out of bed and wrapped her mauve velour dressing gown around herself, she was pleased to notice how calm she felt. This really was going to be the easiest Christmas ever. Yawning, John followed her downstairs to the lounge.

While their parents sat drinking tea, Jacob and Molly distributed presents, chattering excitedly in anticipation of what lay inside. Then the unwrapping began.

"Oh cool, a new ballgown for Barbie!" said Molly, dropping it to the floor and reaching for the next parcel. She glanced across to see what her brother's first present was.

"Haven't you already got one of them?" Molly asked, seeing the Lego police car.

"Doesn't matter, they can have races," retorted Jacob. "You can never have too much Lego."

Meryl threw a knowing look at John.

Molly ripped the paper from the next package, a flat rectangle.

"Wait a minute, these are the pencils I had last year!" cried Molly, pointing to where she'd scratched her name on the tin, unnoticed by Meryl. "And this ballgown for Barbie – that's from last year too. What's going on?"

With a scowl, Jacob revealed his next present to be a remote-controlled sports car.

"Yes, I had this too. Mum, you've just given us what we had last year, haven't you?"

Meryl gave a too-light laugh. "Me? Don't you mean Santa?" She flashed an urgent look across at her husband, hoping for moral support. He misread her.

"Oh, of course, you want your present from me, don't you, darling?" he replied, slipping a pink beribboned box out from its hiding place under the sofa.

Meryl read the name on the lid, spelled out in curvaceous italics, and braced herself to look inside the box. From beneath a pile of crumpled black tissue paper she pulled out a set of lacy scarlet lingerie.

"John, this is exactly what you gave me last year!" she cried out before she could stop herself.

John gazed at her innocently. "Yes, well, you haven't really played with it since then, have you?" he said. Slapping his hands decisively on his thighs, he stood up and retied the belt of his dressing gown.

"Come on, kids, that's just Mummy's little joke," he assured them. "Santa's left your REAL presents out the back. Come with me to the garage and I'll show you."

It was only as John opened the garage door that Meryl detected the sound of two puppies, yapping excitedly as they waited to meet their new owners. She only hoped that they would be brown and white, as Molly had specified on her list.

The True Cost of Christmas

"**I**f I catch your mother doing that again, I'm going to slap her."

Dave looked up from behind the Radio Times' festive film section. "Doing what?"

"Checking the prices on the food packaging in the fridge," replied Marina. "At first I thought she was examining the sell-by dates, which would have been bad enough. But then she reeled off how much I could have saved if I'd shopped at Lidl instead of Sainsbury's."

Dave shrugged and turned the page. "What's so bad about being cost conscious? That's just what my family are like."

"Nothing, if you're the one doing the shopping, but when it's someone else's hospitality, it's just plain rude. It's a criticism, especially when she must realise I'm trying so hard to give her a nice time. I feel like we've got the Hotel Inspector staying for Christmas."

Dave rubbed his nose thoughtfully. "Well, at least she's happy to stay. I'm amazed. She never wanted to before my dad died. And it's perfectly reasonable for her to be a bit more frugal now she's on her own."

"Ha!" retorted Marina. "It's not as if she's got money worries. She's just come back from a Caribbean cruise." Squeezing past Dave to kneel in front of the wood burner, Marina opened up its small glazed doors. "Well, this'll please her. I'm starting a fire instead of turning up the thermostat."

She started twisting sheets of paper from the basket by the fireplace and arranging them into a wigwam inside the stove.

"I saw her looking at the price labels on her presents this morning too. I'd been really careful to take the prices off our presents, but now I'm wishing I'd left the label on the pashmina. Did you hear what she said about it? 'Oh, another scarf.' It's not just any old scarf, it's cashmere. It cost a fortune."

Marina arranged kindling around the newspaper wigwam.

"You look like you're about to burn someone very tiny at the stake," observed Dave, leaning forward. "Hang on, you've dropped a bit."

He picked up a stray strip of paper from the floor. "That's Mum's handwriting," he remarked. "It looks like a shopping list. I wonder whether it's not meant to be for the fire."

Marina took it from his hand and narrowed her eyes. "That's no shopping list, sweetheart. That's a tally of what she's had for Christmas. She's put the giver's name and estimated cost beside each item. And look, she's guessed a fiver for the pashmina! I told you she thought it was cheap!"

She flipped the sheet over. "And here's a column of what she spent on her gifts to everyone else. It's colour-coded. Green if she gave something that cost less than what she received, orange if it cost the same, and red if what she gave cost more."

Dave coughed self-consciously.

"Is that my shopping list, Marina?" said a woman from the doorway, shuffling the slippers that had muted her footfall. "I wondered where I'd dropped it. Can I have it, please?

Marina clung to the offending piece of paper. "But it's a list of this year's presents."

Sandra shook her head. "I need it to plan my Christmas shopping next year."

Marina looked at it again, and suddenly comprehended. "Oh, I see! This is to make sure you won't spend a penny more on anyone than you think they did on you."

Sandra nodded slowly, as if dealing with a simpleton. "That's perfectly reasonable, don't you think?" She stepped forward calmly to take the list from Marina's grasp and left the room, closing the door behind her.

Marina turned to Dave, hands on hips. "Is that how she values her Christmas with us? Is that all it means, the cost of the presents? What about our hospitality and all the other things we do for her, without ever expecting a penny in return? Her lift to and from the station, her special bottle of sherry, the bowl of fresh hyacinths in her room. Doesn't she realise they all cost money too?"

Dave, saying nothing, buried his head in his hands.

"I've a good mind not to invite her next Christmas," said Marina.

Dave raised his eyebrows. "Well, that'll save her a few quid on presents."

Marina threw herself angrily down into an armchair and scowled at the unlit wood burner as Sandra swept back into the room.

"Actually, I've just decided that next year I'm going to dispense with presents altogether," she announced. Marina swivelled round to gaze at her in disbelief. "I'll take you both on holiday with me instead."

Dave grinned and got up from the sofa to give her a grateful hug. "Thanks, Mum, you're the best! We'll look forward to that all year, won't we, Marina?"

Marina did not reply, but knelt silently before the wood burner and struck a match to the newspaper wigwam.

The Unexpected Guest

"Bloody Christmas!" I slammed the window shutters together to hide the view of the zoo and closed the brass fastener to lock out the world.

Three years before, when I'd taken out the lease on the flat, that view had been part of its charm. I often used to use my zoo season ticket, which was a gift from the management to all the residents of this Victorian block that lay next door to the zoo's entrance and was still owned by its charitable foundation. I'd felt as if I owned the zoo, as if it were my back garden, there primarily for my amusement.

Only when Greg and I started to argue did the inevitable background noise start to stress me out. The random roars, shrieks and howls of the animals blended in as part of our rows. I began to feel as caged as they were, imprisoned in a doomed relationship, desperate for the opportunity to escape.

This Christmas Eve, it wasn't the animal noises that bothered me, but the sight of so many humans in festive mood before the zoo closed for the holidays. Beneath the illuminations, hordes of entwined couples and families holding hands roamed about the zoo gardens, whiling away the countdown to Christmas Day with a last-minute holiday treat. Some were even eating ice cream, despite the cold. Even through closed shutters, their shrieks of laughter sailed up through the dusk to my flat, assaulting me like personal insults. Turning my back on the window, I thrust my hands into the pockets of my old sweater dress, suddenly conscious that no-one would be holding my hand for a romantic evening stroll round the zoo any time soon.

***

This time last year, it had all been so different. I'd been down there in the happy throng with Greg, our arms wrapped about each other. We'd exchanged shy smiles as we watched the children queue for Santa's grotto. As we'd patted his live reindeer, kept in the pen alongside, I think we were both wondering, but didn't dare say, how long it would be before we'd take our own children in to see Santa.

Well, that's what I'd been wondering, anyway. Maybe Greg had already been thinking he'd rather have his arms round someone else.

It hadn't helped that my mum had not been exactly reticent about her hopes for us. Over Christmas dinner, she'd been dropping really obvious hints, asking whether there were any dates she should keep free in her new year's diary. When I'd seen Greg flinch at her questions, I'd realised that would be our last Christmas together.

I picked up the remote control, wondering what Mum was watching.

Poor Mum. I hadn't yet had the heart to tell her that Greg had left. It was an anticlimax in the end, but at least we'd parted amicably. After all, it was the season of goodwill.

Although I told my friends that it was a relief to be single again, it was like an aftershock when Greg took away all his stuff. Too fragile to face seasonal drinks with the gang, mostly happy couples these days, I told them I'd be spending Christmas with Mum. But of course I couldn't do that either. So here I was, alone on Christmas Eve, with only a Toblerone and a bottle of brandy for company. Still, what's not to love about Toblerones?

At first it had seemed a good idea to spend Christmas by myself. I could eat what I liked, drink what I liked, sleep when I liked, and pamper myself, all in peace and quiet with no-one complaining. A solitary Christmas would be my self-indulgent gift to myself. It would give me the opportunity to regroup, revise my plans, and relaunch myself looking sensational on New Year's Eve, all fired up and ready to get on with my life. It would be a mini hibernation, begun in the hope and expectation of a following spring.

Now that it was actually happening, though, I wasn't sure I'd made the right decision.

I flicked on the television, inevitably finding It's a Wonderful Life. "No, it isn't," I told the black-and-white James Stewart, and pressed the mute button in preparation to channel-hop. I knew at least one channel always ran a horror film on Christmas Eve to appeal to the defiantly unfestive. I felt that would hit the spot.

***

Just as the mummy was about to get its comeuppance, and I was wondering whether watching a horror film alone had been such a good idea, there came a loud knock at the door. Not the mummy, surely! Or was it Greg? Unsure which of these would be the more horrific, I leapt off the sofa, brushed the Toblerone crumbs off my lap, and sprinted to the hall. I was so convinced that it would be Greg that I flung open the door without checking the spyhole. When I saw who it was, I gave an involuntary shriek.

"Oh my God! I mean, sorry, you're not who I was expecting."

"Well, it is Christmas Eve." Santa's knowing look made me laugh.

"Yes, but I'm not supposed to see you, am I? Not if I want any presents."

"That depends whether you've been good."

With a cheeky wink, "Santa" unhooked his white beard from behind his ears and stuffed it into his jacket pocket. Without it, he looked surprisingly young – about the same age as me. Even so, I could see why the zoo had chosen him to be Santa this year. He had a definite twinkle about him.

"You're calling a bit early, aren't you? It's not midnight for another six hours."

"Late, actually – late finishing my shift at the zoo. They have a rule that I have to stay till I've seen every last child in the queue. They can't disappoint a child on Christmas Eve. At one point it felt like I was going to be there for the rest of my life. When I finally escaped, I discovered my car battery's flat, and all the other staff had gone home. Might you be able to help me out here? Do you have a car? Any chance of a jump-start? I'm sorry to bother you, but there's no-one in at the flats below you. I don't mean to take you away from your family or anything, but I'm getting desperate."

"How do you jump start a sleigh?" I asked, trying to concentrate on his conversation and not his big grey eyes. I'd never thought of Father Christmas as being grey-eyed before. "Anyway, I'm on my own tonight. No family. Not here, anyway."

"Really? So am I."

Realising too late that I shouldn't have told a strange man that I was alone in the house, I grabbed my car keys from the hall table, flung on my coat and led the way downstairs to the street.

"So, have your elves gone on strike?" I asked as we reached the ground floor.

"No, but my wife has. Sadly, Mrs Claus ran off with our postman last summer."

"I guess she's just a sucker for pillar-box red."

I realised I'd been missing this sort of banter since Greg had gone – well, since things had started to go wrong with us, really. Banter is always an early casualty in a faltering relationship, too easily morphing into sniper fire.

I found myself gazing at Santa's red outfit, which hung loose over his pleasingly slim frame. He must have left his padding in the grotto.

"That bloody postman still serves my house, though. He even delivers my wife's solicitor's letters to me. Imagine – a letter to Santa asking for a divorce! How cruel is that?"

Crisp frost on the pavement crunched agreeably beneath our feet. I was starting to feel more festive by the minute.

"Well, you don't have to give her what she asks for if she's been naughty, do you?" I said, looking at him out of the corner of my eye to gauge his reaction while feigning indifference. "That's Santa's prerogative."

Santa shook his head as we reached his smart black sports car.

"No, but I will. That's me all over. Mr Nice Guy."

He opened the nearside door and took out a pair of jump leads that lay ready for action on the front passenger seat.

"Have you got a sticker on your back window saying 'My Other Car's a Sleigh'?" I asked over my shoulder as I went to fetch my Fiesta.

It seemed odd to jump-start a sports car with my old banger, but all the same I was very glad he had a sports car.

Within a few minutes, Santa's car engine was purring gently, and my Fiesta was back in its usual space.

"Got far to go?" I asked casually as he stowed the jump leads in his car boot.

"What do you think?" returned Santa, slipping into the driver's seat. I bent down to speak to him through the open passenger door.

"Should be a clear run to the North Pole at this time of night."

"Fancy a quick spin to warm my engine up? Can I buy you a drink to say thank you before I head to the frozen north? As we're both on our own..."

I didn't need to be asked twice. I slipped into the passenger seat, scarlet leather soft as a warm embrace, and pulled the heavy door closed, a subdued thud indicating its strength. I felt very safe. As I looked down to search for the seat belt anchor, I couldn't help but notice the flimsy fabric of Santa's baggy trousers cascading down to outline muscular thighs. He threw back his hood, whisked off his wig and chucked it onto the tiny back seat, revealing dense close-cropped dark hair.

"So, where to? What's the nicest pub near here? Fancy a night in the Bricklayer's Arms?"

"I'd rather be in Santa's," I said before I could stop myself.

"Well, that can be arranged," replied Santa with a wink.

A cosy festive glow began to course through my veins. I may be twenty-seven, but it's good to know that Santa still has his old magic.

The Unwanted Gift

"But I specifically wrote in my letter to Father Christmas, NO CLOTHES," said Gemma, screwing up into a tight ball the scarlet paper that she'd just ripped off a rainbow-striped hand-knitted scarf.

Sarah wondered how she had raised such an ungrateful daughter.

"Well, maybe he thought you'd been naughty."

They both knew that Gemma, now 12, no longer believed in Father Christmas. Her annual letter to him was really just a shopping list for her indulgent mother to delegate to the rest of her family. Sarah, always keen to take the easiest path in parenting, obediently did so, but felt she could hardly be blamed if anyone went shopping off-piste, or if they chose to make rather than buy a present.

Gemma, as always, was oblivious to her mother's rebuke. "It's far too babyish for me. What on earth does Grandma think I'd put in those little pockets at each end – dollies? For God's sake!" She cast the scarf aside and grabbed another parcel from the top of her heap under the tree. "Anyway it's a bit tight of her, isn't it? She usually spends at least twenty pounds on me. I thought Grandma was meant to be rich."

"Richer than us, that's for sure," said her father, watching Sarah pick up the scarf from where Gemma had flung it.

As Sarah folded it neatly, she noticed how soft the wool was – expensive merino, she guessed, making the big golden sunburst buttons that fastened the pockets at each end seem even colder to the touch. "Look, I think that's Grandma's little joke there, darling: pots of gold at each end of the rainbow!"

"Well, I'm not wearing it. Do you want it? I'll swap it for one of your presents, if you like." Gemma's eyes fell upon an expensive gift pack of nail polish in the latest fashion colours, Grandma's gift to Sarah. Sarah gazed at it for a moment, then shook her head.

"No thank you, darling. When I had my colours done, the colour consultant told me in no uncertain terms that I should never wear brights. I'm a Summer, don't you remember? Pastels, only pastels will do."

But Gemma was already engrossed in reading the packaging of a new computer game that had been listed, in capitals and highlighted, in her letter to Father Christmas.

***

Not long after they'd finished their Christmas dinner, there came an unexpected knock at the front door. Gemma's father Andrew was already dozing in his armchair, and Sarah, who was busy loading the dishwasher, called to Gemma to answer it. Reluctantly setting down her new phone, which she was busy filling with apps, Gemma stomped out to the hall and flung wide the door.

Standing on the doorstep, holding out a small rectangular parcel, was Anna, a girl of Gemma's age who had moved into the house next door a couple of weeks before Christmas.

"Merry Christmas, Gemma," said Anna with a shy smile. "Sorry I didn't bring this round sooner, but we only really finished unpacking yesterday."

Anna looked so anxious for approval that even Gemma's heart softened for a moment. She reached out and took Anna's proffered present, and was just reading the label when her mother came up behind her, drying her hands on a tea towel.

"Oh, hello, Anna! How kind of you to bring Gemma a present."

Anna blushed and smiled, hopping from one foot to another with nervous expectation.

"And I think we've got a little something for you here somewhere too," said Sarah.

Knowing that this was untrue, Gemma turned round to her mother and mouthed "Give her Grandma's scarf."

Obediently Sarah scurried off, leaving the girls making awkward conversation on the doorstep as Gemma pulled wrapping from Anna's gift.

"I hope you haven't already got it – it's one of my favourites," Anna was saying earnestly as Sarah returned with a squashy parcel, its creased paper hinting at its recycled status. Hastily Sarah interrupted, aware that Gemma's letter to Father Christmas had specified NO BOOKS (underlined).

"Merry Christmas, Anna!"

She gave the package to Gemma to hand over, hoping that this might make her daughter look more generous. Anna squeezed it gratefully.

"Cool. Thanks, Gemma. Thanks, Mrs Evans. Enjoy the rest of your Christmas Day." Realising she wasn't going to be invited in, Anna gave a little wave and turned to trot down the path. Gemma had closed the door before Anna had reached the gate.

Sarah sighed. Now every time she saw Anna wearing the scarf – and somehow she knew that Anna would wear it frequently, she was that sort of child – she would be reminded of her daughter's ingratitude.

***

Next morning, coming downstairs in her dressing gown, Sarah noticed a small postcard on the front door mat. Intrigued, because she knew the postman would not deliver on Boxing Day, she bent down to examine it.

The picture side showed a bouquet of Christmas roses above the slogan "Thank you for my Christmas present" in frost-effect lettering. On the other side, in Anna's neat, careful writing, was the following message:

Dear Gemma

Thank you so much for my beautiful scarf. It must have taken you ages to knit it. It would have been one of my favourite presents even without the £10 note in each of the gold-buttoned pockets. What a kind friend you are! If you're free today, would you like to come round to mine to hang out?

Lots of love, Anna.

Sarah stared, open-mouthed. So Grandma had read the first item on Gemma's Christmas list after all: MONEY (highlighted and underlined). She called up the stairs, assuming Gemma would still be in bed.

"Gemma, have you seen Anna's thank-you card?"

Andrew appeared in the doorway of the dining room.

"Gemma's gone out, love," he said, holding out the cup of tea he'd just made for her. "She's popped next door to play with Anna. Seemed rather keen. How nice that she wants to be friends with her at last."

Sarah smiled ruefully.

"Well, it is the season of goodwill."

Good Christmas Housekeeping

U ntil this Christmas, I'd never believed that anybody really used the kind of fancy Christmas table setting that you see featured in every glossy magazine this side of September.

You know the sort I mean. They're always pictured in rooms absolutely dripping with home-made swags of holly, gathered fresh from your vast and well-kept garden, of course. Enormous dinner tables for implausibly large family gatherings sport wildly impractical damask tablecloths, the sort that would never withstand the onslaught of gravy, red wine and Ribena that accompany Christmas dinner in our household. There's usually a breathtaking centrepiece, or even a whole series of little installations running down the table: bonsai'd holly trees; sculptures made from gilt-sprayed pine cones; exotic flower arrangements, each worth about as much as the turkey.

The dining chairs are festooned with gold bows or swathed with tartan. The vast array of cutlery promises at least five courses. Half a dozen crystal glasses suggest these will be accompanied by champagne, white wine, red wine, desert wine, sparkling water (probably Fijian), not forgetting the after-dinner brandy or liqueur.

As to the china, it's either exquisitely simple, price rising in inverse proportion to the degree of decoration, or it's a wittily mismatched medley of vintage Christmas designs, picked up for a song at a little market in Provence.

It goes without saying that in such a setting, the conversation among your most intimate friends and family would be no less than sparkling.

I'm never sure when the hostess is meant to find time to set up such an ornate display. After all, the same magazines usually implore us to start the day with a light but elegant spread of fresh home-made bread, croissants and smoked salmon, washed down with Bucks Fizz (not the sort that comes ready-mixed in a single bottle). They make us feel inferior if we're not also rustling up the most complex combinations of vegetables to accompany our exotically stuffed turkey or goose. Now I'm lucky in that cooking comes easy to me, but I just can't be doing with the rest of it. I'd rather spend more time relaxing with my family than handcrafting centrepieces for the dinner table.

In the odd spare moment, we hostesses are meant to style our hair to perfection, slick on this season's show-stopping festive make-up, and slip into the elegant silk cocktail dress that our perfect husbands have surprised us with, alongside our Christmas stocking crammed with designer toiletries, none with a price tag of less than three figures.

Christmas looks rather different in our household. Even if I were to conjure up such a vision of domestic bliss, it would be lost on my husband Kevin and our ten-year-old son Ben, which is why I was pleased to accept my cousin Moira's invitation to have Christmas dinner at their place. For once I'd be off the hook from feeling a failure for not matching the ideal trumpeted by so many women's magazines.

We'd never been to Moira's for Christmas dinner before, but as this year Christmas Eve coincided with her silver wedding anniversary, she and her husband Douglas had invited all the family to celebrate. What on earth possesses people to get married at Christmas, I wonder. Isn't life complicated enough? It's like choosing to have your birthday on New Year's Eve. A normal person just wouldn't do it.

***

Alarm bells started ringing as soon as we approached their front door, from which was suspended a picture-perfect wreath of real holly, heavy with clove-studded oranges and tartan-wrapped bundles of cinnamon sticks. Matching ribbons festooned the fairy-lit bay trees that stood sentry on either side of the front door.

"At least you don't have to water plastic holly," I said brightly, thinking of our own tatty wreath, which we've used for as many years as we've been married.

Moira shimmered to the door in a silvery silk sheath dress. Perfectly made-up and accessorised, she had not a hair out of place. As it was her silver wedding, I forgave her. Inside the hall, the banisters sparkled with elegant silver-dipped ivy. It looked as fresh as if it was growing there. Glittering above our heads were levitating silver stars, presumably suspended from hidden wires

Once Moira had taken our coats, she beckoned us into the lounge. On a snow-white tablecloth were dozens of expensive delicatessen canapés, displayed like high art on silver cake stands nestling among a forest of miniature potted Christmas trees and frolicking velveteen reindeer. I felt like we'd been asked to eat Narnia.

"Mum, why don't we ever have stuff like this at home?" hissed Ben, seizing three cheese straws in each hand.

"Daddy and I haven't been married 25 years yet," I improvised, false smile plastered on my face like make-up. And there was me thinking I'd done well to buy Ben festive star-shaped Hula Hoops.

The dining room table was no less impressive. To the right of each place setting stood six frost-topped crystal glasses, which I knew from an article I'd just read was done by painting on egg white with a brush and rolling the glass in caster sugar. To frost so many glasses would require a labour force the size of Santa's.

The centrepieces had moved up a notch from Narnia to focus on the openly religious. Silvery angels were doing some kind of synchronised flying beneath an ice sculpture shaped like a giant star. I could tell Ben was itching to break a bit off an icicle to eat, so I held his hand firmly in mine, hoping to look like an affectionate parent rather than a police officer carrying out a restraining order.

I was glad the metre-square silver gauze napkin provided concealed my less than glamorous denim skirt, though I knew I'd be wiping my hands on my skirt rather than spoil the napkin. But I admit I was looking forward to having my Christmas dinner cooked for me.

And that's when things started to go wrong.

"I'm afraid the cream of chestnut soup is just a little scalded," Douglas apologised as he circled the table, whisking away snow-white soup plates. The smoke billowing from the closed kitchen door suggested his explanation was an understatement. "So we'll be moving straight on to the fish course."

At that point a shriek came from the walk-in larder. "Bloody cat!"

Moira appeared in the doorway, fanning her slightly flushed face with a paper plate.

"I'm so sorry, everybody. Barnaby has been a naughty boy with the salmon. Let's fast forward to the palate cleanser. Douglas, sorbet, please!"

Douglas obediently produced from the kitchen a silver salver filled with tiny tin foil tart cases. "Cranberry sorbet," he explained when Ben picked one up to sniff it.

"What's a palate cleanser, Mum?" Ben asked loudly. "Is it like paint stripper?"

"No, that's a different kind of palette, Ben," I whispered. "It's what you eat between courses to get rid of the taste of the last one."

"But we haven't tasted anything yet," he replied at full volume.

Kevin sniggered.

"Please excuse me a moment while I go to carve the bird," announced Douglas. "Or rather, birds. We've got a multi-bird roast. You know, a quail inside a pheasant inside a chicken inside a turkey inside a goose."

"Does that count as cannibalism?" piped up Ben.

As I shushed him, Moira began to set down snow-white vegetable tureens. I wondered what magical mixtures of vegetables lay inside. She lifted the lids.

"Carrot and garlic puree with caramelised onion. Compote of sugar snap pea."

Kevin, normally fond of vegetables, sniggered again. I tried not to gasp at the twin pools of orange and green slime. They looked like the stuff Ben plays with in the bath.

"Are you sure that's not the paint?" Ben hissed. "For the palate cleanser?"

"Chestnut loaf!" said Moira brightly, placing a large red block in front of Ben.

"Is that a brick?" he enquired.

"Saffron potatoes."

"They're exactly the colour of my yellow Playdoh."

Next Douglas bustled in bearing a vast silver platter. The concentric rings in each meaty slice made me think of the cross-section of a tree trunk. This impression was reinforced when I tried to cut into my serving with the only knife I'd yet had occasion to use.

When it came to the Christmas pudding, suffice to say that brandy wasn't needed to set it alight. It had already clearly been in flames, accounting for the loud bang that came from the kitchen just before the microwave timer pinged. Shop-bought mince pies, hastily produced from packets in the absence of anything else that was truly edible, were the only things of any substance that we ate.

"Well, at least we're tackling these with a clean palate," said Kevin in a voice only slightly lower than Ben's.

To be fair to Moira and Douglas, they did keep filling all six glasses, which is why, by the time we got home, Kevin claimed not to remember anything about the meal. I was glad I'd volunteered to drive and felt entirely virtuous raising a toast over the delicious smoked salmon soufflé and tossed salad that I'd rustled up for tea when we got home.

"To the best Christmas dinner I've ever had!" I chinked my glass against Ben's Ribena. "But maybe next year we'd better invite Moira and Douglas to ours."

Past, Present, Yet to Come

I didn't want or need a Christmas present, but Sophie, the young girl whose husband bought the cottage next door last summer, brought me one anyway. In a rush as ever, she came scurrying in to my little sitting room on Christmas morning like a fox fleeing from the Hunt, as if about to take refuge and lie low till they'd passed.

She's always in a hurry, that girl, though at her age – 32 last birthday – she's got all the time in the world ahead of her, unlike me. What with her husband to look after and their first baby on the way, I've told her she needs to slow down a bit. She shouldn't take time out to visit a funny old woman like me.

But I'm glad that she won't take telling, as it's always a tonic to see her. She lights up the room when she arrives, tumbling in through the door. She's got her own key so I don't have to get up out of my chair.

I don't get many visitors these days, just the carers the council sends. There's a different one of those every time, each one looking at her watch and shooting off just as I'm getting to know her. So it's nice to see a familiar face, one that knows my little ways, and I know hers.

It's good to have a visitor who knows to speak loudly and to look at me while she's talking so I can hear what she says. It's tiresome to keep telling those others. Sophie knows to put the milk in the tea cup first, and never forgets to put the cosy on the pot between cups. She always has time to take a cup of tea with me too. These things are important.

She always sits in my visitor's chair, which is opposite mine, beside the window. She settles down snug, then stretches her long legs to share the edge of my footstool. The view out of the window from her chair isn't as good as it is from mine, but that doesn't seem to trouble her. It's lovely to have company that's not on the other side of a pane of glass. The milkman and the postman might wave and smile, but that's not the same.

This morning, after settling down in my visitor's chair – the first time she'd sat down all day, she told me – Sophie closed her eyes for a moment. When she sits back like that, with her long curls dark against the cream linen antimacassar, she looks like a portrait in a frame.

I thought for a moment that the poor lamb was going to nod off (these chairs always have that effect on me too), but then her eyes snapped open, and she leaned forward and took my hands.

"Merry Christmas, Mabel!" she said with a big grin.

She always calls me by my first name, and I've never had the heart to scold her for it. Then from out of her jacket pocket she pulled a slim, sparkly package. She looked awfully pleased with herself, as if she'd just produced a rabbit from a hat, and reached over to place the present gently on my lap. I squeezed it carefully to get an idea of what was inside, before opening it to find a nice new pack of cotton handkerchiefs. (I don't hold with those paper ones.) I've got a half dozen put away for best, but it's lovely to have a better excuse than a hospital trip to start using a new one.

I patted her hand in gratitude.

"My dear, how kind of you to think about a silly old lady when you've got so much else to do," I told her.

My hand rested on hers, looking like a crumpled brown paper bag set down on a fresh white silk sheet. She flushed with pleasure – or that might have been the heat. She always tells me I keep my house too hot.

"Well, it's only a little something, Mabel. I mean, you've got to have something to open on Christmas Day, haven't you?"

Somehow she'd found out the week before that there's no-one left to buy me presents – no friends, no family. I can't think how that slipped out in conversation while I was dabbing my eyes with my old handkerchief and complaining about the hole in it.

"Well, you shouldn't go worrying about me, my dear. You should be saving all your money for your new arrival."

She withdrew her hand from mine to clasp her stomach, round as an apple and full as an egg.

"This time next year, you'll be putting an orange and a piece of coal in your baby's Christmas stocking!"

She shot me a puzzled look.

"And a silver sixpence, that's what we always had, if we'd been good," I went on.

"Next Christmas Eve, I'll be able to bring her in with me to visit you," she said brightly.

"It might be a boy," I objected. "Don't count your chickens."

Sophie shook her head confidently. "Oh no, it's definitely a girl, the 26 week scan proved it."

I just hope she's not bought everything pink. You can't believe everything that new-fangled technology tells you.

"If I'm still here, that is," I added.

"Oh, don't say that, I'm sure you will be. You'll be like my baby's great-grandma."

"Nobody lives forever, my dear, and I'm starting to wear out."

Her eyes filled with tears, so I changed the subject by pointing to a small parcel on the sideboard. I'd wrapped her present in some nice paper saved from the last birthday present I had from my sister, Maud, three years before. It wasn't much creased. I don't hold with this buying of new paper every time you have a birthday or Christmas, it's a wicked waste.

"Save my legs, dear, and fetch that package, will you? It's a little present for you."

She crossed the room in a blur, scooped up the parcel in both hands, pressed it gently and gave it a little shake by her ear, head cocked quizzically on one side.

"I can't begin to guess what it is!"

"Then I'll tell you. It's just a silly old thing I don't need any more. Do open it."

She ripped that lovely paper nearly to shreds to reveal what was inside: an ancient china-headed angel. She looked pleased and held it up to the window to throw more light on it.

"Mabel, it's beautiful. It looks ever so old."

I nodded. "Nearly as old as me, my dear. It's the one Mother used to set atop our Christmas tree every year when my sister and I were girls. I hope you'll want to use it. It's no use to me any more."

Sophie glanced at her watch, then hurriedly rewrapped the angel in the remnants of paper. "But now I must fly. I need to uncover the turkey and turn up the cooker to brown it before my folks arrive for lunch."

She bent down to kiss me gently on the cheek. She's the only person who kisses me these days.

"I'll be back in a couple of hours to bring you a plate of Christmas dinner."

Somehow it had come out in conversation a few days before that Meals on Wheels don't operate on Christmas Day.

"That's so kind of you, my dear. I do appreciate all your trouble."

"Don't get up. I'll see myself out."

It's always such a relief when she says that.

I waited a moment until she passed the window, my hand poised to wave to her as she went down the garden path. Sophie always remembers to turn and wave. Not like the milkman or the postman, or those ladies that come in from the council.

I hope she'll learn to love the china angel as Maud and I did, and I hope it will delight her baby too, boy or girl, whatever it turns out to be. Whether or not I'm still here next year to see it, it's a comfort to this funny old woman to know that there'll always be another Christmas.

A Note to Readers

Thank you for reading **Stocking Fillers**. If you've enjoyed reading these stories, please consider leaving a short review online or recommending the book to your local library, bookshop or friends. Reviews encourage other readers to try my books, and every recommendation helps!

Thank Yous

M any thanks to the author friends who kindly beta read this collection before it was published, and for their wisdom, patience and good humour: Rasana Atreya, Lucienne Boyce, Eliza Green, Linda Hall, Karen Inglis, Rebecca Lang and Veronica Roxby Jorden. Between them they represented readers from four continents to ensure that while retaining my British English, I didn't become unintelligible. I very much appreciate their constructive and thoughtful input. Thanks also to my editor Alison Jack for adding the final polish.

Finally, I should thank my parents for ensuring that my childhood Christmases were invariably happy, even when I hadn't tidied my bedroom before Father Christmas called.

Debbie Young

Also by Debbie Young

Tales from Wendlebury Barrow

The Clutch of Eggs

The Natter of Knitters

***

Sophie Sayers Cozy Mysteries

Best Murder in Show

Murder at the Vicarage

Murder in the Manger

Murder at the Well

Springtime for Murder

Murder at the Mill

Murder Lost and Found

Murder in the Highlands

Driven to Murder

***

Gemma Lamb Cozy Mystery Series

Dastardly Deeds at St Bride's
Sinister Stranger at St Bride's
Wicked Whispers at St Bride's
Artful Antics at St Bride's

***

Novella

Mrs Morris Changes Lanes

***

Short Stories

Lighting Up Time
Marry in Haste
Quick Change
The Owl and the Turkey

***

Collected Columns & Essays

All Part of the Charm
Still Charmed

Young By Name
Still Young By Name

***

To join Debbie Young's Readers' Club mailing list,
please visit her website:
www.authordebbieyoung.com
You'll receive a free ebook of the novelette The Pride of Peacocks when you
join

Printed in Great Britain
by Amazon